Giselle V. Steele

RJ BLACKSTONE

NEW YORK Blackstone LONDON

Fire Lily

New & Selected Poems

RJ BLACKSTONE LTD
A DIVISION OF S&W PUBLISHING
NEW YORK, NY 10020

FIRST EDITION RJ Blackstone August 2019

RJ Blackstone Ltd and design are trademarks of S&W Publishing used under license by the publisher of this book.

Manufactured in the United States of America

Library of Congress Cataloging-In-Publication Data is on file with the Library of Congress.

ISBN: 0-9769949-7-6
ISBN: 0-9769949-8-5 (ebook)

Also by Giselle V. Steele

The Wayfarer's Stone,
Tales of Twilight Dreams

Cold Blue Flame

The Burning of Grey

Rivers Never Fill The Sea

As the dry summer approaches, one flower patiently
bides its time to bloom amid senescing plants.

It lies in wait for an odd but specific flowering cue - *smoke*.

Only after a fire burns over the landscape will a scape
emerge topped with tubular red blossoms.

This collection of poetry is dedicated to the survivors
of the devastating California wildfires of 2018.

While a wildfire incinerates most things, one plant not only
survives but thrives – *the fire lily*.

Contents

SELECTED POEMS

New Poems

The Fire Lily

When the night burns in fire
Amid ungovernable flames
A fury unleashes
That cannot be tamed

Sounds the whip of the blazes
Sounds the strings of a lyre
The gut strings of flames
Of a chaotic fire

And the ashes they're calling
To lay down the fight
But the flames burn intensely
Up to the sky

And the wood trees are falling
A rout to its might
Then rose a fire lily
Against the night

It sprung from the cinders
Between the ember's red light
Emanating from ash
Is the fire lily's plight

Amid a rush of darkness
I saw a gossamer light
In the refulgence of the fire
While the moon was riding high

The glow flickered and waned
As the flames ceded and died
And the lilies appeared
And reached up to the sky

Time Is The Least Thing We've Got

And the days whisk away
And the years never stay

Of all the things we allot
Time is the least of what we've got

Each passing minute is another gone
Each moment lived is a moon at dawn

Seconds swirl 'round each step we take
A piece of life gone with every decision we make

Born to live and yet we die
Each fleeting moment is set aside

And you think somehow you'll get them back
But a shattered vase can't mend its cracks

And the train of time runs on a track
Where future becomes present
Then drifts to the past

After The Sun

After the sun
When the sea is calm
And the light has dimmed
For the moon has come

I catch the stars that fall from the sky
And spread them on the sand
Before their sparks die

I watch them twinkle
I watch them spark
Each edge of crystal
Glows in the dark

And for a moment in time they wait
They live and breathe and to the world acclimate
But just as soon as the skies grow dark
Fire appears, the horizon's monarch

It seems their time to shine is gone
The darkness that breeds them has stopped its song
And back to the heavens the living sparks fade
As the glow of dawn chases the stars away

The Stygian Owl

In these ever changing shadows
Dark as embers when they die
I walk silently among them
As a creature flies nearby

Platinum moonbeams shine upon it
On the path where brown twigs lie
And the dark fog right before me
Shrouds the lake where white swans glide

Once a figure walked beside me
Along the long and winding way
Once a figure dreamt beside me
Yes, here we dreamed we both would stay

Dark the night that shielded shadows
High the pitch of cries nearby
As a creature circled around us
With his piercing stygian eyes

Not a mystery born unto him
But a secret kept inside
Locked away he kept it nightly
Underneath his feathery guise

Through our journey of silent mystery
Our eyes were cast on the stars that slept
Innocent to what was brewing
For the truth beyond was not yet set

Though no words alone were uttered
We smiled with each enraptured step
Unaware of the events unfolding
And deep inside the owl wept

The Warmth Of Wood

The gold of light
From a fevered candle
The sparks take flight

I muse to write
I dream to feel
But all my words
Feel cold as steel

There's something gone
Of once forlonged
A whisper of days
A silent song

Alone I mull
Thoughts in my head
Out stumble words
Down to my pen

But empty words
They can't bring back
The sun to a realm
That's gone so black

Stone Flowers

I walk through a garden near Lake Moraine
To a neglected corner in earth's terrain

Hollowed branches stretch long to find
Some warmth among the stones inside

But they've crafted a pipe dream
And did not know
That was the one dream
They dreamt all alone

Nothing that's now green will not turn brown
Even the bristlecone tree soon won't be found

But the stone flower serves as a paradigm
Something inert can stay alive
Beauty in stone remains for all time

Chasing Moonlight

Passing days have passed on
And stole away the yearning songs
Wondrous days I never craved
For just a thought and my spirit soared

With a resonating hum, a beauty speaks
The gentle sound of earth and trees
Arias swirled by a breeze
The ground vibrates beneath my feet

Sounds around me spoke of whispered days
Light that blinded me one night came my way

Shadows that hid me sought to keep me safe
Art revealed to me a lonely shattered vase

Warmth embraced me
Through the trials I faced
Night intrigued me
And called me by my name

Dreams enticed me with a wish to reclaim
The dawn beckoned me
To chase the moonlight away

After dark comes the dawn
Its melody is a different song
And the dreams not faraway
They breathe new life everyday

Now with every birth of sun
Comes to mind words I'd begun
And with every birth of night
You'll find me chasing moonlight

The Lake Is Deep

The lake is deep
With soundless sleep
It dreams of times
And thoughts it keeps

Time's been long
And days are gone
It turned the nights
Into a song

And now and then
I take my pen
And write of things
I can't forget

Countless words to describe the time
The years of youth set down in rhyme
And I wonder if it's true what's said
That peace is found once it's read

The lake is as deep, as is my soul
In reticent waters it silently holds
The memories that have now
Taken their toll

Just Last Night

Just Last night
I had a vivid dream
In the stillness of night
It took me back again

When I awoke
It felt more bitter than sweet
Because what I recalled
Was just the pain of the bleed

Just last night
I took to wondering
If the blame lies on the fail
Of not being qui vive

Or if the differences that ran deeper
Than I wanted to believe
Induced a flower to sprout early
Antithetic to its seed

Dark Leaves

Dark leaves rain down
On a shadowy lake
Stardust cascades
It's ours to take

But our moves are mindful down to a standstill
For we know the universe does with us as it will
For the sun looks down and it's no surprise
That when we look up our eyes only cry

Strong winds they fan the fire high
Ghostly lakes and rivers look on and sigh
And the red-crested birds take flight in droves
And the sea lions retreat to the rocky cove

Life is the dark leaves that rain down on a lake
As brief as the stardust that cascades on this place

At That Hour

An ethereal glimmer hung over the woods
As the sun's descent dyed the blue
Its red light burned with a fiery mood
Hot but inert as oil it stood

The sky was vastly clear and swept clean
As I stared into the depths of a lucent sea
There, face to face with the cavernous world
I saw fathomless dark with glints of pearl

On the surface of the sea
The boats drifted by
Propelled by the music of the stars up high

At that hour
The clouds sparkled with light
As they celebrated in grand
The emergence of the night

The River Flows

A tiny stream flows downstream some
A mountain slope till it becomes one

Fed by falling snow and crystal ice
Through the land its fingers slice

And the cracks in the ground
Won't hold it back from where it's bound
And the mountains in the way
From its plan won't make it stray

Bet you didn't know
It's one in the same
As the dedicated resolute
That I see in you

Bet you didn't know
That it's just the same
As the resilience in your character
That strengthened and renewed

Through all the trials you faced
It's the depth of spirit that you aced

And from apparent ashes you did rise
What could've been defeat you defied

A feat that is yours to claim
For the river flows in you

Rewrite Time

If I could find
A way to stop
The passage of time

Reverse the hands
That keep their march
And watch the minutes
Swiftly unwind

Words once read
On pages age
And the ink once bold
Begins to fade

But if I could
I would rewrite
The lyrics to
The passage of time

And if I could I'd find
The shrouded meaning
Of the cryptic rhymes

The veil of silence
Sounds barely heard
Another passage
Though long deferred

The secret doors
A compelling lure
That keeps me waiting
And looking out for more

Lessons From The Seasons

The blaze of fall comes with ease
Energy like honey
Drips from the trees

Branches drift down their glittered leaves
Soon they'll be buried in snowy sleeves

Then the earth will lay in repose
That's what winter's breath bestows

Learn from the rhythm by which they live
Concede only what your soul can give

Encase your heart behind strong gates
From there the deepest light radiates

For when the night speaks in solitude
Your private sorrow will obtrude

That Place

When I think of that place
The sun on my face
Blue water I'd trace
As the waves I would chase

The sea's eyes they followed me
The golden sand wrapped around me
A place like this I had never seen

When I think of that place
I retreat inside
The things that I left
Were just things left behind

There's nothing there that calls to me now
Though I still yearn for something
Somewhere and somehow

When I think of that time
Time rushes by
And I'm back at that place
From which in my mind
Has now found a place
Where it can hide

Autumn

Autumn's here
The summer's gone
It left as quickly as it had come

Days are cold now
The woods are still
There's an empty field
That once was filled

From up the sea
Came a floating mist
Rising to the sky
The clouds it kissed

Late afternoon
The clouds fill with light
It shimmers on my skin
As it prepares for night

It's nightfall now
The sky grows dark and clear
Alive come the glitter of the living spheres

I make a wish and blow it out to sea
It's carried there by a zephyr breeze

Autumn's here
Summer's gone
It now plays the tune
Of a different song

Four Bodies Were Found

Four bodies were found
In a seedy area outside of town

On a frigid, dark night face down in a ditch
By a sordid motel for the bogusly rich

Cold and lifeless they lay
Less than 200 yards away
From the place
Where the bonafide wealthy go
To gamble with fate

Among the glitzy casinos and expensive hotels
It appears these four bodies found their personal hell
In the derelict and rundown *Gold Ace* motel
Where rooms go for a few dollars a night
When all goes well
The price is just right

Viridian Woods

Once I ventured into the woods
Where dwell the changeable varying moods
The viridian forest was flourishing wide
Disparaging sounds and blissful sighs
Whispers of the forest to evening skies

I beheld a realm ablaze with hues
Of gold and aubergine within the blue
As a heavenly glow descended to light
Statuesque columns of mystery at night

Glassy lakes reflected inside
The sad and still solitude they fight
Without a sound, without a stir
The immense secret they kept and bore

Then the naissance of snow began to fall
The viridian woods heeded the call
The copper foliage's luster died
And rained a bronze blush from the sky

Then the viridian woods fell ghostly asleep
A profound silence so very deep
The fog appeared in shrouded form
The light returned to where it was borne

Subterranean life shifted and stirred inside
And the frozen woods remained alive

Noctilucent

At the edge of space
In a deep twilight
Dwell tiny crystals
Of water and ice

They appear as streaks
And undulating whirls
Faint and tenuous
Within a sunrise swirl

So ethereal and light
They are seen close to night
Or in the pinkest of dawn
Illuminated by the sun

Rhythm Of The Island

Sometimes in an alcove
A place within my mind
A place I store my memories
I travel back in time

Suddenly I'm there once more
Small white houses with opened doors
And music from the windows pours
A Beny Moré or a Lecuona score

Old enough to know my name
But far too young to comprehend

Through narrow streets of cobblestones
From a distance I see the Malecon
As I hold onto my father's hand
And we turn the corner past the stands

The rhythm of the island
Pulsates underneath my feet
And the jingle from the street vendors
Sounds like musical notes to me

As the sea breeze sways palms overhead
There's aroma of *café* and toasted bread

But now the smiles and faces left behind
Are just memories that we've enshrined
All the while our fate's been sealed
The hardened scars will never heal

As the rhythmical cadence of the island
Sinks into the silence of the tidelands

Perylene Crimson

When I look at the sunset
The colors I see
Are a poet's dream of color
Reflective and deep

Where scarlet is silent
A crimson red speaks
So redolently batiked
Is perylene crimson

It's light and it's weightless
And carries with ease
But when red daubs over shadows
The blues are easy to see

Perylene crimson
A bold fusion of hues
It's hotter than red
But colder then blue

If Prussian blue blushed
It'd be a crimsoned red hush
It would look icy cold

You'd need shrewdness to know
What the shades of perylene crimson's
Melancholy notes connote

Dance Upon The Sea Like A Flame

There's a light that lives inside you
A flame that with the heart complies
It burns incandescent and yet so furtive
That with its glowing sighs it can mystify

This light illuminates the passage
This light defines a space unseen
And if you lost your way by chance
It shines the path on where you'd been

Not a glowing mass of vapor
Like one that burns a candle bright
But a fire deep inside you
That by its rule you will abide

The essence of a soul burns brightly
With just one word it will ignite
And it shimmers like stars at midnight
With a rare and sophisticated light

Like the wildest seas
When energy is freed
And massive waves vie
As they struggle to retreat
Till the sun falls into the sea
With the green-eyed tides

The emerging shades will churn
To allay the intense flame's yearn
And it's a nightly lesson learned
When in your eyes you feel the burn

There are secrets kept like hidden tides
There are feelings that you've learned to hide
And ritually by your will they'll abide

Then when the soft winds blow
And the dying embers flicker low
Your soul will imbue a dimming glow

And you summon out that flicker in the dark
You wonder if the vast sea has put out that spark
But fear not the vapor that to fuel takes aim
And put aside the qualms, put aside the blame
And dance upon the sea like a flame

Elements Of A Sunset

The sun gets larger as in the ocean it sets
It carries daylight's secrets and yet
The sea prepares its vast and empty net

Blue waves scatter and pink shimmers emerge
As the sun soaks up all the light it has to purge
Then it silently falls into the deep sullen surge

If you give your attention to the color of the sun
You'll see foreground images fade into one
As shapes in the night fuse as they're spun

Then a mystery is born unique to every sun's set
For in the darkness there appears
Ambiguous silhouettes
As the sea treasures surface
Caught in the fish nets

Selected Poems

The Hand Of The Poet

The hand of the poet
Lifts it from the realm
Of the tangible world
In which it dwells

He has given a steadfast alcove
For each word a treasure trove
A haven from the lonely streets
Of which they roam

The hand of the poet
Skillfully takes up his pen
He forms a face, a time
And shapes a scene of when

In the bookcase of imagination
Where hidden stories abide
The hand of the poet seeks them out
From the corners where they hide

And he summons each one
A final bow on paper
For a roll in their final reprise

In An Attic

In an attic
Only three feet from the moon
A man stood in silence
As midnight's hour struck its tune

He hung his head
And circled round the table
On the floor his sight was set
For his eyes were barely able
To rest upon the letter
Neatly placed upon his bed

The clock
It ticks away the lonely hours
He stares into space
His mood broods and sours

A knock
His mind recreates the scene
The door unlocks
And a letter is handed to him

An icy tremor runs through his soul
As he smooths the edges of the envelope
By the writing he perceives
Who the sender might be
But the words that are written
He does not want to read

It comes from a woman with golden fair skin
With hair of black velvet
And eyes lit from within

Golden flickers the candle
As he holds the envelope up
And he opens it slowly
To the drumming of raindrops

"She's taken the train
That runs the northbound tracks
It's a shame but she fears
She won't be coming back"

And it's signed
"Yours sincerely"
With an indifferent sort of slack

He blows out the candle
The room is pitch black
The only sound heard
Is the rain's incessant taps

And the moon comes in softly
Through the window with such gloom
As the man sits in silence
In an attic
Only three feet from the moon

The Cave

It was cold
The night moon hung in gloom
Beneath the wind
A strange light came into view

I walked a path of uneven rocky pave
It led through trees to a dark and fathomless cave

I peered inside
Afraid to see
What was the light
Ahead of me?

The stone walls glowed from within
A golden light filled the vast vacuities

And on the wall a moving light
It danced and swayed and flickered bright

I turned to run
But could not see
The path was gone
How could it be?

The rain came on
The clouds were drawn
Torrents of rain
I could not hide from

So I stepped inside the subterrane
As the gloomy night began its reign

The flames they danced in front of me
I was entranced by their luminosity

And as I watched that night
I began to see
The fine line that links
Lucid dreams and reality

The flames inside their warmth I sensed
The rain outside a dream intense

The cave of stone and unfathomed space
The hollowness
I've had to face

The End Of Something

It's a quiet mist filled morning
As I sit and write to you
And as the gray clouds cloak the dawning skies
My thoughts become unglued

And I look out to the roses
Past the window at my view
And I think of words I've chosen
They too wither much too soon

It doesn't seem to matter
To them it matters not
When something comes to shatter
From the glass that it was wrought

And I think about the time that's passed
So methodically through the hourglass
It has trickled down like water
Could life really be so crass?

Summer Rain

A steady summer rain
Falls upon earth's face
But as the silver needles fall
The world doesn't heed its call
And in its mind anxiety
And in its sun, that all can see
A tragedy

Summer rain
That gently falls upon the green
It faintly touches all living things

Droplets that gather as if at a dance
They swirl around the thorns like a lance
Red rose petals hide a surprise
Without a thought they bring reprise

But the world it doesn't heed its call
As clouds from heaven form a wall
They sit on seats of trusting dependability
That the summer rain will always fall

To The Memory Of

To the memory of
A shadowy glade
Of a sleepy place
Of a lure that would bade

To lie beside
Its sliver stream
And its ribbon of sheen
Around lush evergreens

To the memory of
The woods at night
Of its quietude I'll write
Of its burnished torchlights
The home of woodland sprites

They spring upon
The feathery fronds
They whisper their song
And the wind plays along

Faint and iridescent
Like a rising mist
Like a sunset kissed
By the sun's golden bliss

To the memory of
A fools lost gold
He couldn't hold
And now lies beneath
Till time untold

What The Sea Dreams Of

By a shore abstruse and lonely
By a moon that shines so coldly
I watched the sea with its gentle foam
Caress the rocks by where I roamed

A veil of mist of whiteness only
Wrapped round the docks
Where ships stood boldly
Then unfurled its mist around the rocks
Like a tail of fur from a silver fox

From where I stood I felt at my feet
The sea breathe in and the tide recede
Then the imprints waned as they rolled back in

And as I stood and gazed at this dance
Upon the waves the breeze it pranced
They swirled and dipped a hypnotic trance

And I saw the sky and its fiery hue
As the crimson sun sought the freshness of blue
To quench its tongue
And have its coolness imbue
It dipped its face
And the sunset ensued

What are these dreams in the stillness of night
That the sea dreams of and seeks to hide

What is the mystery
The sea won't confide
When alone it rages
And alone it cries
Under the moon's pale orb
And its glimmering light

Words

Several days passed
I could not sleep
A thought slipped in
I couldn't keep
A sudden noise
In the stillness of night
Shattered my thoughts
I flicked on the light

Outside the pane
The wind whistles by
Only a shadow of a cloud
In the late night sky

A name I hear
And I tremble within
Outside the breeze
Sounds like a violin

I sit and I write
But my mood is gone
And when I'm done
I read my words to a song
But the structure's lost form
And the words came out wrong

So I tear up the paper
And remain sitting there
The wind fresh and gentle
Caresses my hair

I stare at the blank page that before me lies
And I think of how a writer's words never die
They appear and they vanish but only for a time
Till the ink's finally won and they're set down in rhyme

The Whispers Of Night

The quiet setting of the lonely sun
Nocturnal gardens wait as one
They draw inside the warmth they find
The evening sun has left behind

Cool and still the moonlight glides
Among the stars and glistening tides
Nighttime blooms in a serene display
And awakens the moon garden's vast array

Arrant bubbles ephemeral and light
Transparent as whispers in the still of night
Evening fragrant perennial vines
Midnight Candy through trellis wind

White that blooms and reflects silver light
Moonraker, White Lace, Impatiens Bride
The Fairy Lily midsummer festival's arrived
Soft muted gold petals come alive

And the faintest puff of sound is heard
As the earth speaks with its reverent words
Between the deepened earth and moonlit skies
The horizon bespeaks the whispers of night

Captive Soul Of The Sea

It was the gloom that was hanging beside
It was the moon as it stared down on me
It was the time of lonesome October
When I was bound a captive soul of the sea

The night quiet and senescent
The wind crisp as it sheared
The fog wrapped its arms around me
The forlorn captive soul of the sea

As I watched the light reflecting
Over crepuscule silky tides
I felt sure the night couldn't shield it
Or the effulgence in my eyes

The mood was dark and somber
As the sauntering tides rolled by
They welcomed in the morning
And lifted heavy, shadowy skies

Then I heard a whispered calling
The slate gray sea I now could hear
What it said I could not venture
Its ocean language wasn't clear

Was it whispering stipulations
Of what this captor needs
To hold me in a dungeon
And hold me hostage of the sea?

I replied: "I must be dreaming,
The briny deep is what I came to see"

But I was mesmerized and diverted
And bound a captive soul of the sea

The Book

The night dark and moonless
As a stranger arrives in town
He rooms in a tavern
Called the *Whiskey Lodge and Hound*

The walls are the color of deep brown lumber
With worn tables that have now lost their luster
And rows of glass bottles some classified as rare
Rising up from the bar the smell of spirits fills the air

The decanters lined up and neatly arranged
Are placed in a patterned chain of array
But the pervasive sense of kinship gives it away
It's not only the bar that shows its display

By the flame of a candle's burning light
The fervor of an old man burned bright
In the middle of the room
He mumbled loud and intense
Saying words that appeared to be without sense

But was it babble and nonsense the old man related?
When most patrons cleared the muttering abated
Then the rest in the room moved forward attentively
Now he no longer seemed to form words incidentally

The old man stood still in the middle of the room
His lined face took on the look of gloom
He began, "Of a certain book it is alleged,
 It does not permit itself to be read."

He looked about the room cautiously
Then eyed a man in the shadows suspiciously
With a cigar in his mouth and ashes falling about his knees
The stranger sat in a corner slowly puffing with ease

Staring at the odd old man
He slowly lowered the cigar in his hand
"And of this book", the stranger began, "what can I do
To have it in my hands?"

The night intensified as did the interest in me
What could the meaning of this book be?

The old man still in his peculiar state
Examined the stranger and his intentions of late
He said, "It is not for the hungry or soulless to see
This book hides inside treasures of mystery
Secrets not disclosed for the average reader to see."

A thick fog hung over the city and a light rain settled in
A loud clock struck twelve
What would the night bring?

The old man walked up to the stranger and glared
He dug into his pocket with calculated care
His old nimble fingers brought something up to the air

It was a note that was tattered and worse for wear
The stranger, surprised, instantly grabbed it midair
He read the note avidly
First the back then the front
But the perplexity on his face still stayed there

He crumbled the paper and headed for the door
Was it fact he was chasing or mythical lore?
Had he left for the hunt or with angry deplore?

Now the clock struck daybreak
With most everyone drunk
And I realized the stranger had set out to debunk
The mysterious book that would never be found
For it was hidden in the mind of one assumed as unsound

Sleepwalker

Like a sleepwalker I roam
Without thoughts far from home
In the early morning rain
I reach the tracks of a lonely train
I see it winding down the way
Wondering where it goes each day
I hear the whistle in my mind
I see the smoke curl into the sky

I imagine a woman sitting on a bench
Her bags are packed, her time was spent
A tear appears and rolls down her face
A lonely woman, in empty pain
Headed for an elusive place
On an empty train

Sleepwalker
One that dreams awake
Take that train to another place
Take some clay off the stone
It doesn't matter to be alone

Nightwalker
You walk then run
With shortened steps you've just begun
To reach a bridge in a little town
A muffled place without any sounds

A town with a roar right through its heart
Under the bridge where the rapids start
Where all screams die on the screamers tongue
And the searching for one will never be done

Sleepwalker be warned you'll never be found
For no one hears them the sounds too loud
In that tiny, dead little town
Where songbirds sing without making a sound

Scotland Moors

Long ago, yes, back some years
Highland rails they took me
Tracks that wound round silver spears
The scent of heather drew me

Soft the wind that swept my hair
Blue the sky above me

And the golden plover's traveled far
Over hills of lilac grandness
And the golden plover sings to the lark
But he only sings songs of sadness

Cold the winds that blow through here
Frost the rocks are embracing
Smell of rain as it clings midair

And then now soon after
The spell is broken

Scotland moors
Its fields wait in the dark
While they sway in the mist
Under the starry sparks

And they bend and wave
Reaching up to the stars
And they pray to feel
The warmth of the sun
Before their time has gone

On The Summer Of That Year

Dark and starry was the sky
On the summer of that year
The air around had a luminous glow
With sparks of fire swirling near

More wood to the fire before it dies
Watch it burn fervent and alive
Just like our reasoning was back then
Unbridled fire with no fears to fend

Smoke rises like burnt offerings
A fragrant, woodsy, exotic incense
Dark trees stretch toward quiescent light
A distant world, latent and burning bright

The sun left its mark beneath the moon
On our skin a glimmer, a burnished hue
And we dreamt of things we were without
And soared above our fears and doubts

We've left behind the summer of that year
Our thoughts now clouded, not as clear
But we still dream of things we'll do without
And soar above our fears and doubts

The Girl From North Bovay

In the midst of an English landscape
Near the village of North Bovay
Lived a girl in a heather thatched cottage
Not far from Winters Bay

A collector of words and people
And in this she found her trade
To write about granite gateposts
And stately gardens with iron gates

In the afternoon she would stroll the inlet
Electing just the right words to say
By the murmur of the bluest spring
With the tree boughs overhead

Every line to the lofty reader
Might be looked upon with dismay
For the air of grief and mourning
Could be inferred as a frivolous foray

She roams the peaceful farmland
That stretches far in North Bovay
And counts up her collection
As she adds new ones each day

Never detracting from her earnings
She dismisses the invidious warnings
As she takes languid pleasure in drinking tea
And delights in scones with clotted cream
In her heather thatched cottage up the way
From the village of North Bovay

He Was First A Writer

He was first a writer
With countless tales to tell
About the sea born expeditions
Where he found gold to sell

His mind unique
To his surroundings
With the wit to read the lines
Between expressions that were written
From a convoluted mind

To maintain his disposition
He rode the stormy winds of time
And the driving rain of critics
That would recite their timely lines

He was first a writer
With a palate for the soul
And the skill to reach the recess
Of the heart's deep, shrouded home

It Must Be The Wind

It must be the wind
I hear in the night
Whispers your name
Then fades from sight

It must be the wind
That brings you to mind
Warm, gentle breezes
That fill me inside

When I awake from a dream
In the still of the night
It comes once again
Through the trees breezing light
I hear it knocking outside my door
I hear it calling me once more

When I open my window
The wind rushes in
Once again I'm filled
With magic from within
That's why I know
That it must be so

It must be the wind
I hear in the night
That magical wind
That inspires me
Then fades from sight

Iron Nights

At nine o'clock the sun goes down
A haze of darkness shrouds the ground
Few stars overhead
And a gleam of moonlight
Dark and heavy is the night

A bewildering tremor
Runs through this place
I walk in silence
The moon keeps my pace

High above me with its glowing eyes
Unveiling its appearance
For the first time tonight

The darkness it whispers
In my ear
My soul broods deeply
It cries a tear

For the stillness it beckons
Emotions from me
As I walk through this land
With such longing

Be still and catch a gleam of light
That rises against the northern sky

In this melancholy place
That moves one by sight
At the time of the year that brings
The iron nights

The Wayfarer's Stone
Tales Of Twilight Dreams

To the reader:

This is the narrative of the wayfarer's stone
Penned in the days of twilight dreams & tales
Written with the sound of whispering tones

It was late evening
The sun was gone
But it's warmth
It's gold
Still lingered on

The heavens declared
An infinite calm

Hollow tones and trembling sounds
Here stands the poet looking around

The stars they danced before me
Then quietly took a bow
Alone I was left till the morning
When words of expression I found

I picked my words as if gathering bouquets
I chose the rhyme
The music to play

I collected shadows for all to see
Tales as deep as the fathomless sea

Some are letters, some are thoughts
Others mysteries that struck the heart

So, put out the lamp
By the gray light of day
Read on through each line
To the final page

Of the Wayfarer's Stone
From the cobblestone path
Of which I roamed

Tales relinquished
That turned into gold

The Wind and the Sea

Today alone by the sea
Tides opened earth's inner soul to me
A mist lay thick reaching up to my knees
And now and then, a soft breath of wind

Today alone by the sea
My memories escaped their captivity
They wandered back to a certain day
To a place and time so far away
And now and then upon my face
I feel the wind as it gathers its pace

Today alone by the sea
I remember the time and of this I dream
With thoughts in fact that I do not fight
With these memories of mine
That have now aged like wine

And at these wistful times I succumb to write
In my mind thoughts take flight
About that ambiguous time

And now and then a breeze sweeps by
Making sleeping mists rise and sigh
They hurl and fall
As the stormy seas begin to call

Today I happened to be by the sea
Today I happened to be remembering

The wind is calling, do you hear?
The sea it beckons to bring me near
The sea is calling out to me
The wild and wind swept sea

The Summer Sun

Lilac colored flowers
Centered on long stalks
Reaching to my knees
As through the fields I walk

The sea foams gently
Up against the rocks
A veil of sound emerges
From seagulls by the dock

The summer sun
That shows its face
Looks down and smiles
Upon this place

Small whitewashed houses
Against deep blue sky
Green grass just sprouting
Their blades supple and alive

Sometimes I look at the grass
And see
The blades of grass
Looking back at me!

At times it is so clear to me
When I look in the skies
The image I see
The summer sun
That shows its face
Looks down
And smiles upon this place

The Raven Of Ivory

Said to be completed ten years after death
The stony gray tower was the tallest one yet

The poignant tall figure
That at its long windows stood
Now looks out of the pane
With despair and gloom

And every night at its turret by the gold-dipped moon
Perched a raven on the periphery of a windowless room

Not nigrescent in hue did its feathers unfold
But as white as a snow owl or so the tale's told

This raven of ivory the only friend by his side
As strange and unique as the place where he'd hide
Stoic and cold it never takes flight
The raven and the man subsist identical plights

Their fortress of stone where they live all alone
A place where the heart and thoughts have no home
This figure a figment of notion it seems
This man is as isolated as the raven he sees

Some might deduce a double life he does live
A twin entity of sorts but only one of them grieves

For each evening a light in the turret burns bright
A candle whose flame lives deep into night
And a man stands alone looking up at the moon
His eyes like the raven's in the windowless room
Encased in the fortress of stone like a tomb

The Candle And The Scribe

Two unlikely friends
The candle and I

Two unlikely friends
The flicker of a flame
And I the scribe

And of what do my confrere and I write
As I sit and stare at the dance of light?
From expressions of love to expressions of hate
Of time that's passed, that came too late

Words that come to me I've amassed
To form a bouquet of words of the past
These words I write they quiver and sigh
From the start of a dream to the last goodbye

Seas that restlessly toss their waves
High into the flames of a sunset's rave
Words I've collected, words I've enshrined
For these rare flowers I found are mine

The candle's flame waits in quiet repose
Until the last letter set down in prose
Dies on my paper crestfallen to dry
Evoked from the inkwell in which it hides

Two unlikely friends
The candle and I
But of this amity though odd I find
No better friend in which to confide

Castle Of Gray Stone

She wrote about a castle
A castle near her home
A stony fortress in a wooded place
A castle of gray stone

At this moment
It lay lifeless
The emerald sea below
Its waves would roll in softly
Commanded by the moonlight's glow

The stones they hide the castle
In the deep part of the woods
And there exists a garden
Where the tallest primrose stood

Among the sundrops in the snow
A girl walked past them all alone
She'd watch the evening sun unfurl
Vincent's colors across the world

A mysterious figure
In a misty place
Sprinkled with glitter
It is there she waits

A white figure in a misty garden
Winding through it a path of stone
And every night the footsteps leaving
Are yet a mystery unknown

Atlantis

An island nation of noble cause
Born of the magic
Of what seems a thought
Rings of water as aegis took root
To guard the dwelling the princess took

But born of such vapors
Could love hold back
The rage of the ocean's ardent attack
North were mountains which soared to the skies
Where a chariot's winged horses were ready to ride

Bittersweet memories and tearful lore
By the side of the sea many of them were poured
How deep! How deep! Is the fervor of their sleep
The dreams they dream tonight they won't keep

And in the morning with the sun's arise
Silence will fill their throats inside
For during the night's high, burly tides
They were swallowed down to the deep inside

On The Dark Side Of The Street

On the dark side of the street
Lonely eyes meet
People smile sweet
But it's a smile that's weak
On the dark side of the street

Everyday news
Of a shooting star's shoes
Marked in cement
And millions are spent
As they sell there charm
On the 10:00 o'clock news

But lately at night
The feeling's not right
You're lonely and blue
And you haven't a clue
It wasn't quite as you thought
What else in life can be sought?

Money and fame
It just isn't the same
As you once had dreamed
It's as dark as it seems
When you're shoes take a walk
On the dark side of the street

A Muse In Lotus Land

The coming of the sun, the moon, and stars
The celestial lights flash gleams of sparks

The coming of the spring
The snow had gone
The jeweled birds sang peregrine songs

In the woods outside a lonely town
There's a silver lake where fog circles round
In blackberry winter they rise from the ground
With sparkles of dew they're often found

Mysterious blossoms that rise like incense
These nonpareil flowers with a hue intense
Their inflorescence a lotus with a lavender blush
They are nurtured at dawn when all is hushed

In the midst of this vaporous garden of blooms
A sprite-like figure by the water's gray gloom

Among feathery willows and river rocks
A muse graceful and slender lithely walks

In lotus land where the sun rains gold
Where fairytales of fantasy are often told
A reverie of thoughts fills one's head
A tale that's evanid once it's said

Spring In London

A wind filled day
And within my mind
My thoughts at play

I'm in a land of architectural fame
A city where nothing is the same

A garden park in the city's eye
Statues of stone set by the lakeside

An artist's brush dipped in watercolor gray
Washes the antique city on a cloudy day

I open my window
The smell of wetness seeps in
 Not far off in the distance
The sound of a sweet violin

The notes seem to linger
High above the red rooftops
Until a thunderous crash
Shatters the crystal notes up

Then as fast as it rose
It's gone
And the London air
Is once again calm

That's how it is
In this land of imperial fame
In this city
Where nothing is the same

A Taste Of Rain

Night has fallen
There's a drizzle of rain
Thunder's exploding
I peer out of the window pane

Outside I'm walking
I hear the dirges of a train
My lips are moving
And I taste the rain

The cold sets in me
Iciness through my veins
I look above me
And on my lips
A taste of rain

The Forest At Midnight

 It was a year
When the forest rustled everywhere
And the exotic cries of painted birds
Sprinkled magic in the air

Even the cool blue waters that fell would know
That midnight had drawn near

The whirring sounds of mayflies and moths
Mingled in the forest as they flew back and forth
Their whispering sounds was all that I heard
At midnight in the forest as it spoke without words

For three nights alone I could not sleep
I was entranced by this forest so dark and deep

And whenever midnight's shadow drew near
Alive grew the forest gently whispering in my ear

These few days that passed through
Their passing was a sight
My only friend was the forest and its solitude at night

And when from my memory these days I retrieve
I see how strangely these nights affected me
In the dark, green forest so late at night
With its gentle murmuring at the hour of midnight

Into The Transparent Blue

Into the vast emptiness of a transparent blue
Cutting through waves disappearing from view

A mysterious figure within shadows glides
A poet has come to watch the turn of the tide

Between us there was the bond of the sea
The mysterious figure, the poet, and me

The sun sank low and where it once glowed white
Now a deep flushed red replaced the bright

And the mysterious figure sparks the curious to ask
A merman, a maid, or manatee perhaps?

Within the crowded ocean full of memories of men
This figure perhaps could be one of them

But the poet is real, his eyes glow with a light
As in his mind, he lives the creations he writes

Forsaken dolphins to the edge they come
While the sensitive poet looks solemnly on

Engraved in the depths of my mind is a song
I seek out its meaning though it has long since gone

The mysterious figure, the poet, and me
And the ambiguous ocean of faded memories

Where aquatic relics are entombed in a grave
Of a watery realm with nothing left to save

Want To Go?

Want to go kayaking?
         To you
                  Said I

We'll fly down the river beneath cloudless skies
And coast the sweet waters where jasmines align
The fragrant path we'll take
And time we'll defy

Want to scale a mountain?
         To you
                  Said I

We'll watch long strips of water
Stream down the sides
Of rough crags and mountains
Carving stone as it glides

Want to catch stardust falling?
         To you
                  Said I

We'll feel the twinkle of glitter
On our faces at night
And the glow from the fire
That keeps us warm inside
Will keep our hearts beating gently under moonlight

Want to go on safari?
         To you
                  Said I

We'll explore secret caves
Where marine life hides
And scour pristine waters
Where mantas glide by
We'll spot coral gardens
Teeming with reef life

Want to hide in the jungle?
      To you
         Said I

We'll lay on the rich green velvet
Of the jungle at night
We'll live life in rhythms
And set the tone for the rite
Then the realness of life
And contentment we'll find

Winter's Morning

A cold, gray winter's morning
A pale blue light was dawning
As I headed down the roadside
To see where it would lead

As the darkness brooded round me
Scattered leaves were falling softly
Floating, silently to my feet

High above my head came a rustling
Distantly, a tune was humming
I stopped to listen closely
But the tune I couldn't pick

Snow had fallen steadily through the night
Day clouds hung heavy, not a ray of light
The day grew dark and misty
As I turned down another path
I walked a trail of icy rain
Where bare barked trees collectively framed
An old abandoned rustic train

Sounds slowly grew around me
And I became aware
Amid the noise of passersby
Of a man's presence standing there
He stood a while and didn't move
I felt my blood go racing through
I gathered strength and turned to see
and was shocked by the sight that awaited me

Not a soul around for miles was found
Not a single noise, tune or sound
Only the lonely track of footsteps
On the icy winter's ground

Wandering

Gone are the days
Gone are the hours
Gone is my soul,
It left restlessly
Where are the dreams
That I so believed in
They faded like mist
Over the darkened sea

Memories escape me
Floating on breezes
Back to a time
It left wandering

Walking the same streets
Seeing the same scenes
Feeling the same, though
Now numb to the pain
I see a pair of eyes
But they look through me
I feel their stare
Though they're not really there

Gone is my youth
Never to renew
Gone are the years
They fade effortlessly
Where is the time
That I so guarded fast
The clock's ticking sound
Is heard faintly advance
A dismal tune set
For a desolate dance
A wandering, stumbling,
Faltering stance

The Wayside Inn

A man sits outside of an Inn
His cheeks are hollow, his face is thin
His hair is sifted with flecks of gray
Like the sky above him on a thundering day

At first sight he seems on in his years
But his eyes tell he's not the age he appears
His hired coach waits nearby the inn
He sits and stares at his drink of gin

Slowly and calculating he begins to write
Not a poem or song, but a letter of goodbye
He has trouble beginning—finding the right line
He closes his eyes and sees her face in his mind

Heavy and dispassionate begin his words
Such bitterness, he thinks, he's never known

And the inn's owner bewildered, calls out to him
"Hey buddy, haven't you had enough to drink?"
But he's deaf to the call and too numb to think
He looks up at the sky and his eyes grow pink

And the sunlight hides beneath a veil of gray
As the night drives out the last light of day
And the man sits until dusk and then dawn again
Unaware he could use a listening ear and a friend

There is nothing singular about this man or day
The same scene's repeated but in different ways

The story the same with a plot just as thin
With diverse characters and the same brand of gin
By the side of the road at the Wayside Inn

Surrealistic Imageries

Surrealistic imageries abound
Where the silver moon dipped in gold is found
In the crystal woods with its gleaming trees
You'll find silver barks with crystalline leaves

The skies are waves of melted gold
And silver strands into clouds they mold
A sapphire river ribbons around
Jeweled stones with a rippling sound

Beware for the onyx panther stalks
Whomever he senses through his forest walk
With emerald eyes he watches the woods
And guards the garden where diamond petals bloom

If you should find yourself in this place unseen
Don't try to wake for it isn't a dream
The sparkling dust in the veil of fog
The ruby brilliance on a jeweled log
These images the mind's eye can only see
For they're only surrealistic imageries

On A Deserted Highway In The Still Of The Night

On a dark deserted highway
As midnight's moon drew near
My car engine's humming
Was all one could hear

My eyes grew heavy
And hypnotized
I longed to reach a place
For the night

A light drizzle began to fall
It spotted the dust on my car that's all

The window was blotched
And I couldn't see
What was that figure ahead of me?
It looked like a woman in the dead of night
I flashed on my high beams to catch her in the light
Her dark cloak shimmered as she faded from sight
And a light rain kept falling in the still of the night

I slowed down my pace
When I reached where she had been
I peered intently
To the woods deep within

But not a sight was seen
Of the woman in black
And I drove on wondering
If I should have turned back

What if she wanted to warn me
Of danger ahead?
What if she wanted to advise me
Of where this highway led?

I glanced in my mirror
No one in sight
And a light rain kept falling
In the still of the night

Up ahead a dark winding curve
With a sign that read,
"If you can read this sign,
 You'll soon be dead!"

I slammed on my brakes
My wheels screeched with fright
My car swerved half-off a cliff
But held tight

My heart raced with fear
As I let out a breath
Staring down the dark abyss
I could see only death

An electric buzz sounded
And my lights flickered off
My mind contemplated
How swift I'd be gone

And I stared down the cliff
For its depth was a sight
And a light rain kept falling
In the still of the night

Above A Sea Of Fog

I'm drifting above a sea of fog
Beneath me are white clouds of mist
Silently floating above the place
Where I found no way to exist

The ocean of pale I now call home
Within my mind I call my own
A place I find without this need
To my thoughts and heart I will concede
Those memories that I release
To breach their captivity

From the recess of my soul
Locked behind a guarded wall
As above a sea of fog I float
I think I hear you call

Beneath me now I hear my name
Although the sound is not the same
As many years ago

Floating silently in my space
I see the outline of your face
Within my mind your features I trace
Delicately with fingers of lace

I travel here inside my mind
Tranquil days I hope to find
Leave details that have me bogged
And venture to a sea of fog

The Moon Lily

When the moon lily blooms
And calls upon the blackest gloom
It blooms as a last breath of fall
As winter's crystals begin to call

Shimmering petals of sliver white
They illuminate fields among shadows of night
Adorning winter with what pertains to spring
The moon lily's scent a heady fragrance brings
To the darkness, a glowing light
To the shadowy glade that deepens at night

These flowers they need the moon showers to grow
They open at dusk to drink moonbeams from below
The iridescent cool light in their petals they hold
And unleash a radiant glow when they unfold

Shadow Of A Dream

Walking in the shadow of a dream
Transfixed by this secret deep within
At times in utter darkness
At times in glimmering light
I keep a watch on this dream of mine

I kiss the air
It tastes of wine
This is my reverie
A sole bliss of mine

In the shadowy woods
That keep this dream
Twinkling lights cascade
From deep within
They fall like glitter into its depths
As the sultry heat looms like incense

As I walk in the shadow
Of a dream that is mine
In a mystical forest
In a world out of time

The Seaside Village

The intense blue sea crashes on the shore
Of a seaside village of old folklore

At six o'clock the village floods with light
I sit outside and await the night
A cat stretches out on an old blue chair
By a village tavern his customary lair

A frail old man takes his daily walk
Down the cobblestone street to the seaside dock
A violinist greets me with a bow and nod
Then strikes a chord with a smiling façade

I sip my wine and watch the passerby's
If only I could slow the fall of night

I hear the whispers like filtered sunlight
The auburn-haired girl comes here every night
In a café by stone fountains she sits and waits
But the lonely sun's descent seals her fate

And the whispers follow her down the cobblestones
It will be another night spent alone
As I stand to leave I think of that girl
Who does she wait for as her years unfurl?

In this seaside village of old folklore
Where the intense blue sea
Echoes on the shore

The Moon

The moon it drifts on a misty haze
Suspended above earth's vibrant maze

If the moon could dream
Would it dream alone?
And if evoke it could
What hopes would it hold?

The moon it looks to the earth below
Its silvery shine holds tales untold
It holds the key they seek to find
But will never grasp for their eyes are blind

The moon it glides on velvet skies
It stretches its moonbeams far and wide
In a vast darkness in silence it sits
And of things it's seen it cannot speak

For the ignorant seekers
The future is bleak

The Old Captain's Rum

Many tales of the sea have been told
Many sails have sprung up in search of gold
But only one, and this one, is a dark mystery
Of the old man that lived in the tenebrous sea

He was pale and his bones showed well from his age
Up in years but with no fear
He'd wrestle the sea's rage

He had one friend he thought true
That was frivolous but bold
And he sailed the seas with the old man
In search of the gold

Every night when the ship docked
At some distant port
His friend would bequeath him
A dulling of sorts

He'd sit at port's side and smile with his friend
As the clanging of iron waved flags overhead
And they'd talk and they'd whisper about the wet gold
How much would it fetch when cleaned up and sold?

But his friend just sat there quite motionless
A warmth could be seen
But with a stark bitterness

Not much could be said of this camaraderie
But a dangerous friendship
Born from the sea

And the old man was blind
To the damage being done
He couldn't let go
Of this insidious one

This secretive friend
Not a person or being
But a tasty diversion
A complement to a feeling

Then one cold lonely night
You could hear the boats rock
The smell of sea air filled the waterfront

And if you listened real closely
And your senses weren't numb
You'd hear a faint reveling, drunken hum
As the old man drew his last breath
And took one last slug
Of the captain's dark mystical rum

Twice This Dream

Twice this dream I've had
I'm alone at sea
The crescent moon it strings
Strands of silver beams

Farther from the shore
The distance I ignore
Footsteps leave behind
Prose on the sands of time

Chains that toll against the sterns
As ships sail by their torches burn
The smell of salt is in the air
The burdened wind stirs when it dares

Faint ships hidden in darkened fog
The meaning of this mystery lives on
Into the deepness of depth unknown
Into the seas where wild waves groan
So deep it's hidden from all eyes to see
Little hope to figure its mystery

Twice this dream I've had
Of this part of the sea
And the moon's secret dance
On the feral cerulean seas

The Victorian Harbor

The harbor was still
Like a blue mother of pearl
Huge rocks were the clams
On its tongue was a pill

The sky was serene
And lovely at dusk
Molten gold streams were left
By the descending sun

And in the harbor
Waiting for another day
Were tall black flagged ships
Now put away

The lights flickered warmly
To announce the arrival of night
Soon the sound of shuffling
Of the shoes of those strolling by

Men nodded and glanced
As they smiled with their eyes
Women blushed as they passed
And walked on through the night

That's how life was then
In this Victorian harbor town
When the sun descended quietly
Alive came the night sounds

Wind Swept Night

One wind-swept night
Upon the shore
I stared into dark earth's very core

Green tides receded
Sharing its depth
I dared not look away
From the secrets it kept

High up above me
The golden stars soared
The constellations told tales
Of ancient lore
They spun and whispered
As neutrinos formed

Down to the earth
Down to the waves
The darkened seafoam
Reached the caves

One wind-swept night
Under moonlight
I searched the skies
Where I looked to find
A way to track
The passing time

The Ship

A flash of blue like sapphire stone
A glint of gold …what do these waters hold?
I peer inquisitively into an infinite deep
As my equilibrium I try to keep

On the edge of the ship
The wind blows cold
It cuts and nips as a pirate's whip

The bow and stern trussed and secure
Cut through the raging water's lure
I watch the ship's mast rise and fall
Plunge and dip into a watery wall

Wild blue waves that dance below
The wooden vessel's polished gallows
They form the water curls of the sea
Mysterious tresses untamed and free
They dance and fling themselves up to the sun
And resonate a whispering mermaid's song

A flash of hue as nighttime fall
Scintillating star lights begin their call
The arms of the docks open up nearby
And await the return of the ship with a sigh

The Realm Of Silence

Rain falls softly on cobblestones
A distant thunder sounds alone
Lips that form words unknown
The soundless world they call their home
Is within the realm of silence

A smile dictates the words they say
Silently they seem to wait
But no response was ever made
Within the realm of silence

Expressive eyes communicate
Tacit words they never state
They speak with stifled words unheard
And in their world they sit alone
Within the realm of silence

Ice Flowers

Ice flowers that congregate
Among the glitter of snow they wait
Hidden, rare and so alone
Their fragile stems hold their own

Against the howling winds and rain
Against the blizzard of snow in vain
For a streak of sun will melt away
All their strength, in just one day

And there they'll stay
Ice flowers only in name
Beauty that will never be the same

A love that grows here in this place
Emits a light
A translucent blaze
Hidden and rare and so alone
The fragile heart holds its own

Against the silence
Against the night
Against the loss in the lonely fight

And a glance from his eyes
Will melt away
All the strength that it's fought to gain
And there it stays
Left to weaken with a lover's gaze
Like the ice flowers strength
The beauty of this love
Will capitulate

The Friesian

What is that sound?
It echoes around
A clap, a click
A thud so distinct

The strength is heard
In the svelte line of the curves
The hoofs
The flex
The mane
Wild and unkempt

Dark as indigo
With almond eyes
They glow from within
A determined stride
Its vigorous restraint
Its spirited breath
The speed of its run
Is feared by some

The Friesian's black velvet
As dense as night
And its long flowing mane
A rebellious demonstration of might

Golden Seas

The golden sea
It hides inside
Life's mysteries
In its tempestuous tides

Never ending motions
Appear outside
But in its deep
The stillness hides

Unaccounted treasures
Many seek to find
Dreams of glory
And greed in mind

But as the seas
Vast waves roll in
It carries only treasures
It desires to give

The precious ones
It guards inside
With monster waves
It keeps its eyes
On all the secrets
One could find
If one possessed the keys
To open up the golden seas

Fame's Last Call

The cold winter's moon is shining
The cold winter's moon is blinding
The cold winter's moon is showing
The cold winter's wind
That's blowing

Sleep now
Inside warmth is hiding
Sleep now
Winter's day is dying

Come now
Evening's light is shining
You'll find solace here
Soft as downy

Feel now
Winter's wind is biting
Don't heed
Brutal gales like lightning
Come stay inside
Until the dawning

The moon
It drops pearls of light
On the wet streets
At night

It rains a light
At night
It rains a glowing light
A distant bright

A man he walks alone
He walks among the passerby's
And when he looks into their eyes
They're hard as stone
They drop their eyes avoiding him

And after all
All that he's reached
Reached the peak
Reached so high
But now the lines are forming
His face, the years, the tears they're showing

And I think of things once said to him
Fame's not made up of golden strings
It's just a thing

And those that you've come to trust
They'll wither your soul for fame's empty lust
Their heart as cold as ice won't see
The person you've come to be

And all that you've reached
You reached with a sigh
Half with pleasure, half with strife

But heed the warning
Yes, be advised
With each breath you draw
From deep inside
With fames last call
A part of you dies

A Liquid Sea Like Silver

A liquid sea like silver
Motionless under moonlight
Slate-gray waves amalgamate
With shadows in the night

It's framed by darkened crags and cliffs
That encircle and keep inside
The mystery it holds within
Those liquid silver tides

Slow and calculated
Like lambent silk it glides
With disconsolate, intense yearning
It flings itself with might

As it releases its downcast spirit
Deep into night
Its liquid silver coalesce
Under the cool moonlight

Then the mystery is still again
Locked away from prying eyes
Fathoms down and deep within
Enigmatic silver tides

Blush Of Twilight

Gold silk paints the sun's arise
Soft waves of the blushing skies

I see morning light
Softly brighten darkened skies
While I stand alone

The pale golden light
Marks the end for all the nights
I try to find
A place to hide inside
While I lay staring at the lonely sky

I summon dreams I'd left with yearning
The stirred emotions I'd left burning

But then honey days turn twilight
I am once again wrapped in night

And I'll lie awake
Just envisioning your eyes
And their peacefulness inside

Do You Believe In Love?

Do you believe in fairytales?
Do you believe in love?
In prancing, winged horses?
And snow white graceful swans?

And when night acquiesces to the starry skies
Do you believe those stars that shine
Are polished diamonds up above?
Do you believe in love?

And when you see fresh fallen snow
Do you believe that deep below
There's a secret world kindled aglow?
Do you believe in love?

Do you believe in fairytales?
Is of simple love all that you tell?
Do you give your heart as pawn?
Do you wager love for fun?
Do you believe in love?

For when the brisk autumn winds
Swirl fallen leaves of gold
Do you hear its rustle call?
And when sweet music fills the night
Does it scintillate your heart
Does it stir? Does it light?
An incandescent spark of life?

I believe in crystal notes that on billowy clouds float
I believe in love

I believe in the glow that to a soul it brings
I believe in the peace that fills one from within
Yes, I believe in fairytales
I believe in love

And in the power both possess
To exonerate a somber soul
And send it soaring high above
As swiftly as a flying dove

Forest Of Dreams

For the first time that night
I entered through the castle door
And climbed the staircase
To the second floor

I heard a buzz of voices
Coming from within
My heart thumped loudly
I knocked and stepped in

The vast room was dark
Barren and alone
I looked around searching
For the voices I had heard
But no one appeared
Not a voice not a word

Then a flutter of wings
Burst from the garden below
At first I was startled
By the sound unknown
I looked out long windows
And saw geese take to flight
Their outline was dim
At the hour of midnight

They were looking for shelter
From the upcoming rain
Just the same as I was
When I walked through the gates

What castle is this?
Why is it alone?
I had stumbled upon it
When the forest I roamed

The wind sang through the trees
That stirred lightly that night
I looked out to the forest
A strange glow from a light

The breeze filled my head
Like the smoke of incense
And I followed down paths
Without logic or sense

This forest of dreams
Where gossamer wings take flight
It captures the wanderer if only by sight
And seizes the thoughts
That exist there and binds
The illusions within
The eye of one's mind

A Tribute To Grace

She held herself with grace and style
Lace and tulle draped for miles
Lithely she walked down the carpeted aisle
Nodding acknowledgment to the royal smiles

A woman of beauty, the poise of a queen
Such mode and confidence that came from within
A glow that emitted from her serene eyes
A light the same as the winged fireflies

And as she knelt at the altar that day
A princess she turned, in a magical way
Unsure and unaware of what lay ahead
She gathered her dress and through rice showers fled

No one knew how sad was her fate
No one had flashes of her unconscious state
Pulled from the wreckage of her car one day
And how her enchanted life was to cease in this way

The princess beloved most never knew
The little girl within her that never grew
The charm and her beauty, a thing of the past
Fairytale lives, it seems, never last

With The Last Light Of Winter

The last light of winter
Reflected brightly on that eve
The last flakes of downy
Landed softly on the leaves

Soon would come the dawning
The skies draped in golden streams
And with it, its quiet stillness
That echoes emptiness within

With the last light of winter
Gone are crystals on the ground
With the last light of winter
A snowy blanket won't warm me now

If I had some way
To keep winter here
I'd walk among iced trees
Keeping my dreams near
And in the snow they'd never find
A shattered dream
The broken bind

On Waves Of Sleep

A white blanket covered the woods
To warm up the roots
Of the slender black trees
Multifaceted snowflakes
Twinkled glitter off its leaves

The swirling air embraced
This frozen place
The snow it gleamed
Like silver lace

Underneath the blanket of snow
There's a curious world kept below

It is hidden beneath so deep
Drifting on waves of sleep

The magic fog that settled in
The moonlit night sought refuge in

As the woods dressed up in winter
So cold and deep
And drifted on waves of sleep

The Desolate Sea

The wailing wind
Sweeps by my ears
I sit amid these sounds I hear

Far out I see the fishing boats
People boarding for places
In their winter coats

The sea flings itself up
Foaming into the air
Then tumbles and tumbles
Without a care

Here I sit warm and dry
In a hidden reef
Watching boats sail by

A small white boat's sprung a leak
But steers out to the wind
With a moan and a creak for the heed is weak

I lean back on a wall
And remember the dreams
Of the storming surf with its raging seas

And the mysteries of the blue
That are concealed in the tides
They are hidden from eyes
And trapped inside

A bird swoops low
It has caught its prey
A boulder breaks
Not far away

Loose rocks roll down into the sea
As a soothing feeling steals over me

The smell of wet earth
Comes up from the ground
As the gathering raindrops
Start falling down

Like long silver needles
They drive into the ground

The rain descends around me
As the oceans rise
And I fall deep asleep
And the same dreams arise

The same ones that haunt me
And won't set me free
Like the stormy tides
Of a desolate sea

The Mysterious Man

The old man stared at her while she spoke
Things had been the same since she awoke
Without the comforts of a dry sleeping place
No rest had come to his somnolent face

"Where in the woods can I find him?" she asked
His silence was followed by a sip of his flask
He shook his head slowly from side to side
His solemn face gave the reasons he'd bide

He said, "Go twenty one days toward the sun's descent,
And if after this, you're still intent, your time was well spent
For you might hear his name in the village there"
Then he lowered his stare

His eyes fixed on the fiery camp blaze
Taking a stick he poked at flames
Some of the embers had already died
That's when she noticed an odd mist in his eyes

Then through the smoke's haze
His voice emerged as if from a daze
"Somewhere in the forest, perhaps not far away
His tired eyes await the moonrise each day"

And as at the fire he stared
He continued to talk unaware

"This man that you seek pursued remarkable trees
With glints of gold dust hidden in their leaves
One morning in fall he traveled north to a stream
There in the blue waters he found
Golden leaves just floating around
So it was there he set his camp

With few provisions and a lamp
Among the uncanny dwarf trees
He remained till time deemed.
Then winter rain turned to snow."

He again shook his head
As one does with worry or regret
And he stared out to the darkness
And he spoke with a dread,
"After some time in the spring
They found an ax and some string
But the man you now seek
Was never heard from or seen"

And just as the fire gained might
Rain began steady and light

The old man leaned back on a rock
And his eyes shifted up
The hot fire hissed at the drops
That rained without stop

And as she stared at his face
His features she could now place
His weary eyes now seemed to smile
A familiar twinkle that resembled a wile

At this scene of ambiguity
This tale ends in obscurity
Now the reader must decide
Why did this man seem to hide?

This tale to some might seem wild
Or insane at most mild
In his avaricious hunt, you choose
Did he unearth a find only to lose?

The dwarf trees with leaves of gold
The mysterious man of which it is told

And who's the old man that by the fire sits?
A forgotten poet that has lost his wit?
Or a lovesick knight
With an irrevocable plight?

Whichever the deduction taken by you
You've unwittingly lived this tale
Of the search you'll live to tell
That led one to doom

The Wind Calls Your Name

There's a place
Where the wind calls your name
Sometimes it whispers
Sometimes it's tame
But at times in a whirlwind
It unleashes the fray
And the wind howls your name

In the depth calm of winter
When all is still and alone
A shivering wind passes through here
A crystal wind so cold
It cuts its way through the trees
Playing and rustling with the leaves

And then I hear that sound again
Bringing back thoughts of when
All my plans now seem inane
That wicked wind's to blame
The winter wind
That calls your name

Under The Stars

Under the stars
On a moonlit night
The midnight sea
Is bathed in light

The echo of its waves
Reverberates in my ear
I catch dust from a star
And wish to bring it near

Under the stars
I take to write
In depth of winter
Or in summers light

And the brilliance before me
In the glowing sky
Could never seize the magic
Or its grandeur belie

And as the bright
Fades softly from sight
The raindrops fall silently
In the night

Under the stars
Pure diamond moonlight
Until the next dawning light

Twilight Cadence

Into the deeper blackness
I dared
How did I come to be here?
I remember walking alone out there
In the night-time vaporous air

That strange misty gloom
Of the woods at night
Hung low and solemn
Under the moon's lucid light

The woods were full of countless
Strange shapes
They emerged from the night
Like shadowy black capes
So still and dark
Yet their silhouettes so stark

They moved amidst the foggy swathe
With a vague quiver
Like a great winged moth.

I listened intently
To the rhythmic night-sounds
The vibration resounded deep from the ground
It snaked and encircled
Around dark green trees
Their profoundness brought some unease

From the faintest lisp to the softest trill
Nothing was still

From the deep booming and piercing cries
There was an echoism far and wide

And the bright, dancing fire
It spoke in my ear
Its fantastic fire language
Which meaning was clear

Its flames mesmerized me
To the point I feared
Of which no release was near

Twilight cadence beckoned the way
To a mysterious night with an uneasy stay
Until a glow brought the next dawn of day

The Sea Castle

I walk through a forest of strange trees
Bamboo, mango and tamarind
Teak, salt trees and rubber plants
Have I reached this place by some enchant?

A veil of sea mist from the ocean's tide
Swirls into the forest with a shadowy glide
In the fog I see images of wondrous things
Thunderous horses with transparent wings

The wind whispers a name as it brushes by me
on the water's edge a reflection I see
A stone gray castle of marble and slate
Statues of gold guard its gates

The sun blinks once and night time blooms
The stone fortress glows by the glimmer of the moon
Goldstone and quartz shine from door to door
Underneath ruby velvet carpeted floors

The sea castle it sits on a desolate hill
Dark fern shrubs grow outside its sills
Its magnificent gardens where shooting stars grow
Are lined with mulberry and lavish mangrove

And every night beneath ink-blue skies
Dark ocean waves crash near its side
Though cold and alone it seems to be
A stronghold that holds life's secrecy

For the sea castle's a vision only a heart can see
And a safeguard for those looking to find peace

That Magic Day

The night moves on
So swiftly
And through the darkness
The light shines so dimly
So gloomy

There was a time
When the light shone so bright
It broke through the night
Those days the sun rained
Its sparkling light
A deep golden sight

Light windy days were filled
With a magic
One could feel

The rays they danced
Up in the sky
Gold rays of light

And when the wind swept clean
The horizon with might
Clouds were imbued with golden light
As the sun bowed low
Into the sea at night

Sunset

The light began to weaken
As the sun sank low
The sky glowed with fever
A red and amber afterglow

The sea waves stirred before me
They dashed against the rocks
Like a mermaid rising from its depths
Curled white sea foam were her locks

Then soon the sky took on a hue
Of a velvety, satin midnight blue
The sun had lay down for the night
And now the sea had calmed its fight

Radiant facets of the stars appeared
Brilliantly shining so crystal clear
But the moon's watch soon would end
And the glittering of the stars would fade
When the morning sun shone again

The Music Of The Soul

The moon it sits in darkness alone
As moonbeams scatter pearl drops aglow

If only one could string these pearls to show
Their beauty in clear glass enclosed
But this gift won't be known

To some their beauty is never shown
Such is the music of the soul

Imaginary gardens where fragrant flowers bloom
Cinnabar red and mulberry hues
Flecked with gold and Persian blue

It's hidden in a fantasy deep within
Immortalized in a dream of gold
Muse induced wishes never told
Such is the music of the soul

Rhythmical beauty of words untold
Ignites the flames of fire to provoke
And sings in solitude sweet sounding prose
And paints a portrait in life's canvas

Though
To the world it won't be shown
Such is the music of the soul

Nightfall

The twilight is glooming upward
Out of the corners of the room
The shadows of furniture grow taller
As night time calls in gloom

At first the shadows grow deeper
As they start to lose array
Then they lose distinction
As objects lose their outline to gray

The shadows creep across slowly
Over each corner of the room
In the center an inert figure
Sits among the soundless gloom

Fainter and fainter grows the light
As umbrae swallows up the bright
A double handful's measured out
And dark has been scattered about

The figure is now wrapped in sable air
For the blackness has replaced the fair

There is no sound in this dark unknown
Only the slow ticking of a clock
And the old house creaks a bemoan
An unintelligible sort of knock

And now the figure sits invisible
Within the blackness of this room
With only the rustling of silk curtains
As the wind blows in a tune

The northwest wind
Has swept the sky clear
In the sky a stroke of dark appears
Deep clustering foliage
Flutters in the dark
A broken twig leaves its mark

Through the branches of the trees
There sifts an effectual light that gleams
A silvery dance upon the branches
Of the wet and darkened leaves

Moonbeams fall aslant into the room
They play about the darkened gloom
Nothing has stirred
In these hours of brume
Not even the figure in the dusk-filled room
Only the hands of time sound their tune

Here the meaning of midnight we find
A frozen waltz of light and darkness entwined

The Gilded Rose

I awoke this morning
A fine mist in the air
I walked to the garden
As if summoned by a dare

Tall trees hovered above me
Dark leaves clung to their barks
Fog set in around me
Suddenly the day became dark

Walked over to a clearing
Just some wood twigs scattered about
Then I saw among the brown leaves
Out of the ground something stuck-out

Centered on a stalk
There it stood radiant and grand
I knelt down beside it
And tried to take it in my hand

A gilded rose
A sight to see
Golden petals
On dark green leaves

I looked around but there was no one in sight
Drawing closer I grabbed the stem tight
But as soon as my fingers wrapped around its leaves
The rose closed its petals in retreat

I stood there watching
As it faded from sight
Back into the earth's garden
Into another world's paradise

Enchantment

Daylight has closed its eyes
And awoken the dark-eyed night
The sable cloak of evening
Is wrapped in flickering lights

The streets lay dark and lonely
Wet cobblestones glisten in moonlight
A cold stiff wind is howling
Tall dark trees shiver in the night

Not far off the sea is churning
Molten silver and emerald green
Huge waves pound on mysterious shores
Filled with diamond dust that gleam

The ships that sail to these islands
Are rocking on the sea asleep
For night has fallen with enchantment
Into a slumber magically deep

Into The Arms Of The Sea

Alone again this snowy night
Walking the streets of golden light
You feel the cold whip by your face
It stings the same as your heart aches

The sound below you've come to know
Cold rain, brisk wind, and crunch of snow
The mottled smoothness of its glow
The scene seems painted by Van Gogh

When are you coming back
Do you know when?
From that cold void of black
Will you be back again?

Pale light that burns into the night
Along the street you search to find
But icy windows are shut up tight
Impervious to the winds harsh blight

When is the time that you will flee
From that cold void of black it's come to be
When are you setting out and breaking free
Into the open arms of the sea

Let go of all you know and fear
Surrender to what you once held dear
Let go of that universal sphere
It's easier than it might appear

Come don't wait, it's clear to me
The case is opened to make your plea
Concede yourself to what you foresee
Into the waiting arms of the sea

On The Underground

Voyage on the underground
A stony fortress I have found
A maze of foreign faces here
Dart about with no one near
It coils around so dark and deep
It holds the secrets it must keep

Never knowing what is found
Voyage on the underground

Travel here it takes you there
To the point of where you dare
Drops of water keep their mark
Against the stone they look so stark

And when your eyes they blink away
From the brightness of the day
Then you'll know that you survived
That murky tunnel that few abide

And somehow you became unwound
By your voyage on the underground

Morning Rain

The sky is dawning
It's lacking golden splendor
My heart is yearning
To see the sun again

Outside it's calling
The wind is rising and whirling
Like wings of winged horses
Under restraint

The morning rain
Dances on the window panes
Gently it falls
Not knowing at all
The lonely notes it plays

I hear the rhythm
Its hypnotizing tapping
I close my eyes
It echoes in my heart

Another day
I see it die before me
Another lonely one

The morning rain
Awakens a numbing pain
Gently it falls
As loneliness calls
To the feelings I cannot refrain

Little One

My little one
He loves such boyish things
Race cars, turtles and dragon wings

Though a test to my patience
I often find
Those muddy little feet
With a smile so kind

Nothing can turn your life upside down
As a pint-sized hero running around

Your dress belt
Is transformed into a whip
Your sofa becomes a battle ship

At the end of the day
When he climbs into bed
I wipe the sweat from my brow
And think of the next day ahead

A tender kiss goodnight
A flick of the light
My little one
Drifts off to dream
A sweet dream tonight

The Ivory Tower Of Dreams

It stands stark against the midnight sky
Tall and carved shadowed by light
Formed from the purest alabaster white
A refuge for the ones with a worthy plight

Two caryatids among the six
On the *Porch of the Maidens*
On the Acropolis

The August moon ablaze with light
Reveal the details in the columns at night
The stars they sing their mysterious sound
That reach the catacombs deep underground

From a swirl of wind these towers were formed
The catalyst, a zephyr left from a storm
As the nocturne proclaimed diminished sight
At the edge of darkness in the realm of light

And if your fingers do trace these tower's ingrain
On these pillars of ivory you'll find countless names
Of those who once sought a refuge it seems
In the evanescent ivory tower of dreams

Flaming

Flaming red sky
The sun stands still before me
The gates open for the night
The horizon is ablaze with light

The time has come
And I will sleep no more
In my mind
I hear a knock at the door

I look about there is no one there
Into the dark I wait and stare

I had seen his eyes
I had heard his voice
One sleepless night
There was a rustling noise
I went to seek him in the dense of night
A slender candle gave off golden light

I spoke his name softly
But was afraid he'd hear
I went searching
But was afraid to find him near

I walked alone through leaves of gold
Stepped lightly over logs of moss and mold

That night I dreamt
An unsettling dream
It summoned to me the face I'd seen
I tossed and turned
I was afraid to wake
And face another day
My soul unslaked

Dark Isle Manor

A noble house stands
On the Yorkshire Moors
Profound secrets are hidden
Behind its stately doors

A colorless day in 1801
Behind a gray veil are the rays of the sun
A stay for the night a tall man assumes
Is ready for him and he signs *nom de plume*

He removes his gloves slowly, surveying the place
His beguiling appeal hides the deepest heartache
A torrent of rain has forced him to stay
In the place of his torment, he has tried to allay

He's taken attentively to a chamber for the night
And warns not to call him until the break of daylight
Coldly and brooding the fireplace he lights
Then ignites a pipe and stares into the night

The pungent smoke curls and rises dulling his mind
Soon he's dosed off in a dream deeply entwined
Someone's at his window he can now recognize
With long hair that's golden and dark angel eyes

The figure motions to follow to a garden beyond
He sits up startled unsure to respond
Then the image fades softly as he wakes up at dawn
Broken and tormented his will all but gone

This dream at the manor not rare or unique
It recurs every night when this man falls to sleep
Time away from this place did not bring relief
For he returned from his journey skeptical of his belief

Now the cool light of dawn brings dreaded unease
When he realizes his anguish, he cannot appease
For regardless the dwelling or place he may be
In a break from reality this dream will repeat

An Image Of A Boat

I find myself thinking of a an image of a boat
On turbulent seas it sets afloat
A crescent sail of blue silk it wears
It flaps against the rough wind it bears

The skies they seem so far away
The ocean's arms fling up in dismay
A secret bond with the seas stirring tides
In its deepest waters, the moon's secrets hide

Mysteries of death, there hidden in life
Among the reefs concealed inside
Within the sea's opaline guise
As the moon commands tides fall and rise

And the small white boat it gently glides
As the horizon glows crimson in the skies
Stealthily it moves into the deep-blue night
And fades in dark silence from evening light

Black As Raven

Black as raven dark as night
A nebulous mystery obscure
Shapeless in daylight

In darkness here
It exudes its light
A shimmer of brilliance
That fades at midnight

Not man but beast
With intense might
Where no eyes can see
He evades the light

Within his soul a fire that burns
Within his radiant eyes
A deep smoldering glow

The power of torrents
Its rider does know
His rage and spirit
In his grasp he holds

Through mist and fog
The rider breaks toward the bog
Down wet cobblestone streets
As torchlights flicker on

As midnight approaches
Not a sound just the trod
And the clacking of hoofs
As the rider rides on

Cold Blue Flame

I will wait
At least a while
Catch my breath
Before my words beguile

I weakly sigh
Then take what's at hand
My adviser is a candle
Its glow devoid of command

The flame's appearance
Striking in its hue
The deepest of its refulgence
A cool lambent blue

The ice-blue flame
Composed and serene
A betrayer of thoughts
Though poise is what's seen

And now as I write
The evening sky wears on
A grim solitude ascends
And looks quietly upon

Through the windows of this sorrow
Through windows of despair
A moonless night in spring
Imbues a sadness in the air

The Enchanted Light

One morning it rose behind the trees
An enchanted light, a glowing gleam
It hung over the earth with a silver sheen
Over fields of gold, over ice blue streams

The sun was one
To bring to life
The peaceful forest
That slept at night

The horizon itself was clothed that night
In a mauve and gold shimmer of light
A celebration underway in the peaceful skies
In grand style the stars reflected wide
Below to the ocean's gilded tide

The moon was one
To bring a tune
Of rejoicing song
At midnight's bloom

An enchanted light like fantasy
Danced with life iridescently
On petals of satin violet sheen
As the earth displayed its opaline
Deep in the forest unseen

Twilight Mystery

Somewhere in the shadowy depths
An effulgent twilight mystery is kept
In the deep of forest and still of night
Strange curious creatures take flight

Graceful and glowing
As living lights they're bred
In the night sky are trails
Of gossamer threads

What mysterious origin does this lambent glow hold?
What secret do they carry within their winged glow?

Once I sat by the fire and a refulgence appeared
It flew up, circled about, and landed very near
The heat I thought would drive it away
And in the cool dark flowery world it would stay

But this night wanderer defiantly circled in flight
And landed aglow in the deepness of night
Feathery and sylphlike it rested upon the leaf
Of the great palm's branch at the top of the tree

Then it must have assumed I'd imprison its light
For without warning the winged creature took flight
Into the blackness of jungle, into the night
To stay a luminous mystery of the forest at twilight

The Storm

A storm rips through a fragile town
The ships are docked their sails are down
The wooden decks once so strong
Now sway and cede, tattered and torn
Tall ships abide the oceans commands
As the wind whisks up the recluse sand

In restless shadows the moon awaits
It watches over the little town's fate
Like a soundless maiden its beauty beams
A platinum silver from its rays stream
On starlit waters the winds will die
And leave their mark with a merciless cry

The storm's fast rise, a blessing and a curse
It sweeps through its path strong but terse
Till the winds stronghold gives out its restraint
And the rains pour down solemn and gray
The harbor town awaits the glow of day
It endures the time to come alive again

Then the sounds will grow slowly up from the ground
A bustle will flourish from whispered sounds
From the clanging of ships as the sails hoist up
To the Friesian horses' familiar clop
Unlike the stars that watch so serene
From within the night sky, an iridescent queen

Close My Eyes

I close my eyes and travel
To a distant place and time
Where a gold blazed afternoon
Seeks refreshment in blue skies

And the sea it laps up gently
To the old, worn wooden boards
That frame the pier's enduring skeleton
That stretches out long from the shore

And the warmth it wraps around us
As it burnishes our skin
A deep, gilded glow of summer
That penetrates within

To the recess of our minds
To our very heart and core
And every wave that breaks before us
No longer strangers of the shore

As the hands of time keep moving
We're unaware of what it means
Of the dreams it quells before us
Of how wasteful is its scheme

The familiar smell of ocean
The warm sand blankets the sea
We find peace in this one notion
Within our eyes we see our dreams

A Man Of Mystery

Along the seas of Mélange Bay
Among the romance of its woods in May
Stirred a shadow by the water
Of a steel-like gray

There were many stories
Of this secretive soul
A real maritime mystery
A narrate for the bold

Some thought it a man
Of a lonely existence
Still others a peasant
With no hope, they insisted

All that was known in all certainty
Is the hour he'd appear furtively
Before light revealed him
By the night-veiled sea

At times he'd stroll the boardwalk
With an uneven gaited walk
A cane to keep his balance
And a hat to keep out glances

And there he would stand
Looking out to the sand
And to the dark mystery
Of the lonesome sea

The First Frost

A delicate breath passed over the blossoms
Like icy lace it covered the moss
Fall had taken a stronghold
With its first frost

The flowers they stood at attention
Not giving in to the icy wind's intentions
Stubborn flowers that refuse to die
Though their time is up
They still face the sky

Grass stems stand stiffly
up towards the sun
Fallen leaves skim on the ground
As lonely ones

The roses are flushed with fever
Scarlet red and ruby hues
It's the hour of fall
When everything turns new

Yes, fall is here
Settling everywhere
Inward deep

And on each plant
A sparkling frost
A mark embossed
Of a long winter's sleep

The Town

I opened the window and looked out to the street
It was quiet and hushed
The roads amassed secrets to keep

Not yet quite midnight
The stars twinkled bright
They hung high in the sky
Without a cloud in sight

Far down the road a faint mumble arose
Rumbling noise from town as the taverns closed

Undulating echoes from faintness to loud
A steam train's horn blew in sound
Its haunting whistle chimed with smoke as a shroud
As through the town's heart it plowed

This town boasts grand appeal
But I had suddenly lost my zeal
And to now sit and write
Seemed more and more like a fight

A summon from oceans not far away
The cobblestone path led me astray
And my mind journeyed down the steep steps of the town

When I reached the wild seas
The moon beamed in ecstasy
Not the wind or salt air
Heard the wave's whispered dare

"Come dip in cool sea; come seek out your dreams
But realize this truth; not all return once they do"

I shivered from the cold and made my way back to the inn
I sought to forget where I had just been

A gold light flickered onto the street
Wet cobblestones were beneath my feet
Back safe in my room all was gray
Just shadows of things put away

A half-closed window let in the night
Like a darkened fog that steals one's sight

Perception took in every inch I could see
The whole room became very clear to me

From the moldings above the vestibule doors
To the detail of red tiling on the floors

So I closed the window and locked the door
And sat back down at the table once more
I pushed aside papers not seen to the end
And I took up my pen…

"I shall write about winter and the fluting of a train
And the great darkened seas without refrain
The cobblestone's luster under the light,
How they glimmered like gold among shadows of night"

And time passed through without making a sound
And the day's cloak was fog roundabout

I finished my story without further delay
My companion the moaning of a lonely train
And then came the time round back again
I knew staying much longer would be inane

So I packed my bags methodically
With shadows I had found
And left behind that mysterious town

A Mystery And A Dream

A moon hue of hushed violet and pearl
On an ocean's mist that rises and falls
A pirate on a treasure hunt's untold tale
Of the fanciful capture of a great blue whale

A lonely isle in an emerald sea
An aestival sky looming over me
The stars dream beyond the sapphirine cast
Mute and motionless I view the vast

The sea wind whispers to each star its name
The sun's rays sprinkle down a lucent rain
Radiant pools collect seaside
Sated with living jewels
As the warm sand cools

A mystery and a dream
A mystifying fantasy

But what is a dream if not love first felt
And what is mystery if not life itself?

A moon hue of hushed violet
Dims to a shadowy gray
A night light burns not far away
Quiet and still earth's expanse stays
Chasing away the last light of the day

The Birth Of Night

Sunset clouds
Fill with light
Like glowing embers
About to ignite
Vibrant orange
And violet hue
A wash of color
An electric blue

Soon the evening sky appears
A change of wind
Blows crisp and clear

A whirl sweeps up
Leaves on the ground
Bronze and gold
Twirl all around

And the sunset clouds
That brimmed with light
Now a muted gray
As they fade from sight
And bring to earth
The birth of night

The Docks

The docks lay quiet when you first walk up
It's cold and gray with a thick heavy fog

Large ships lie sturdily
On swaying waters below
Surveying them closely
You would never know

Just how fragile they are
For their solidity's a disguise
Since when they take on water
Their sturdiness dies

The seas in contrast command the world
The waves are restrained from a sudden unfurl

The sand with its golden fingers caress
The groundswell's potency under duress

As the dock lays quiet under the winter's sun
The warmth from its pale golden rays barely none
And at night black ships coil their knotty ropes tight
Portholes scintillate with gold flickers of light

The clanging of iron is all that is heard
As the seas churning waves speak without words
They sway and they hurl against the moon
And the dance of midnight into daylight blooms